THE
LOLLIPOP
MONSTERS
Christmas

ERIC T. KRACKOW

Illustrated by Eric T. and Heather M. Krackow

Schiffer
Publishing Ltd

4880 Lower Valley Road • Atglen, PA 19310

Designed and Illustrated by Eric T. Krackow
Layout Design by Danielle D. Farmer
Type set in Everyman/Mountains of Christmas/CastleT

ISBN: 978-0-7643-4743-6
Printed in China

Published by Schiffer Publishing, Ltd.
4880 Lower Valley Road
Atglen, PA 19310
Phone: (610) 593-1777; Fax: (610) 593-2002
E-mail: Info@schifferbooks.com

For our complete selection of fine books on this and related subjects, please visit our website at www.schifferbooks.com. You may also write for a free catalog.

This book may be purchased from the publisher. Please try your bookstore first.

We are always looking for people to write books on new and related subjects. If you have an idea for a book, please contact us at proposals@schifferbooks.com.

Schiffer Publishing's titles are available at special discounts for bulk purchases for sales promotions or premiums. Special editions, including personalized covers, corporate imprints, and excerpts can be created in large quantities for special needs. For more information, contact the publisher.

Other Schiffer Books by the Author:
The Lollipop Monster, 978-0-7643-3773-4, $16.99
The Lollipop Monstesr Meets Clem the Kluz, 978-0-7643-4287-5, $16.99
Bill the Snowman, 978-0-7643-3219-7, $16.99
Have an Abominably Good Day, 978-0-7643-3496-2, $16.99

This book is dedicated to
God, my family and friends.

One wonderful winter day in the land of Monstoria, the sun began to peek over the horizon, and Larry the Lollipop Monster slowly woke up from a long night's rest.

He let out a big yawn, then rubbed his sleepy eyes. Through his window, he could see the snow-covered trees.

Larry jumped out of bed to get a good look at the beautiful snow-covered land. He was very excited, because today was Christmas, and his friends would soon be arriving to celebrate this very special day.

He went into the bathroom to brush his teeth. He was so excited that he almost forgot to rinse!

Then he went downstairs and put out some mugs and filled them with hot cocoa and milk. It was the perfect Christmas treat!

Next, Larry went into the living room and lifted the lid to his old-fashioned record player. He placed the needle on the record, and the joyful sounds of a classic Christmas song filled the room.

Christmas wouldn't be complete without some fresh-baked cookies. Larry mixed the ingredients for his favorite recipe, and then put the cookies in the oven to bake.

Suddenly, he heard a knock at the door. Larry stepped out of the kitchen and raced to the front door.

He already had big smile on his face because he knew who was waiting on the other side of the door.

"Merry Christmas!" everyone exclaimed. Clem, Zabby, Jagger, Xue, Xola, and Sanford smiled and waved at their friend Larry, and he wished them a Merry Christmas, too.

Larry opened the door wide and let all of his friends into his warm and cozy home, where stockings hung above a roaring fire.

His friends loved all his festive decorations, especially the fresh-cut tree.

Larry went to the kitchen,
and brought back the cups
of hot cocoa.

The cocoa was delicious, and his friends drank it up as fast as they could.

Larry grinned at his happy friends, then turned in the direction of the fireplace. He noticed that it could use a few more logs.

Larry told his friends he would be right back, then slipped on a warm coat to go outside to fetch some firewood.

He went around the side of the house and came to a stack of logs. But then he smelled something burning. He looked around to see what it could be.

In the distance, Larry saw smoke rising from the forest. He decided to go take a look.

Larry heard a sound that grew louder as he got closer to the smoke. He peeked around a snow-covered tree and noticed a monster sitting on a log trying to stay warm by the fire.

As Larry got closer, he realized that the sound he was hearing was the monster crying. Larry wanted to help the poor creature.

"H-Hello?" said Larry. "Oh my!" the frightened monster said. "Is this your firewood? I'm sorry...I was just trying to stay warm. I'll leave right away!"

"No, please stay," said Larry. "I was just concerned...my name is Larry. What's yours?" The shy monster nervously responded. "My name is Walter," he said. Larry shook his cold hand. "Nice to meet you. So, why are you out here?" he asked.

Walter's face grew sad again. "Well, I just get sad this time of year. Ever since I can remember, I have always been alone on Christmas. Everyone else seems so happy and joyful. But I have no friends and no family."

Larry was a kind soul. The thought of someone being alone on Christmas made him sad, too. He knew just what to do. "Well, that needs to end today, Walter," he said. "This Christmas you won't be alone."

He sat next to Walter on the log. "How about you come over and meet my friends at my home? There's food, cocoa, a tree, and a warm fire...what do you think?" he asked. Walter could tell right away that Larry was a kind monster. He happily agreed to join Larry and his friends.

The two monsters put snow on the dying fire to make sure it was out, then set off toward Larry's home.

As Walter approached Larry's house, he noticed the beautiful Christmas decorations. "Wow!" he said. "I love the pretty lights! This must be what Christmas is all about."

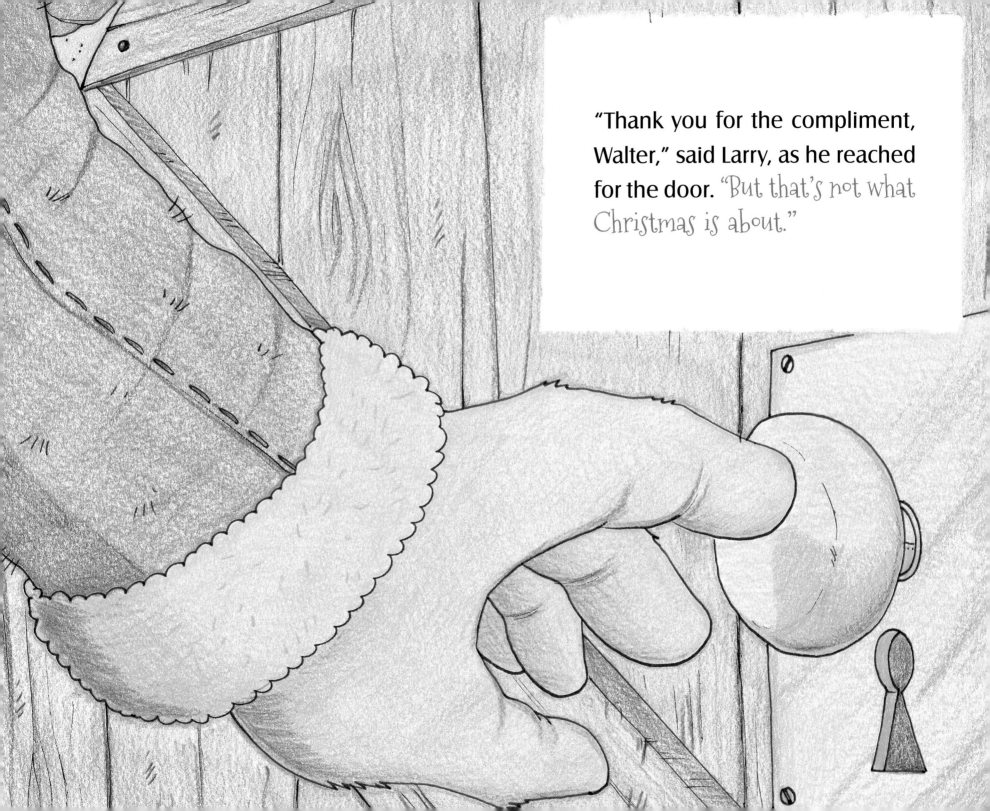

"Thank you for the compliment, Walter," said Larry, as he reached for the door. "But that's not what Christmas is about."

Suddenly, the door swung open, and Larry and Walter were greeted with the warm smiles of all of Larry's friends.

Larry introduced Walter to everyone. "Nice to meet you!" said Jagger in a deep, monstrous voice. "I'm Jagger, and this here is my purple-haired buddy Clem!"

Zabby was next. "Hello, Walter. My name is Zabby," she said. Walter reached out and shook her small hand. "N-nice to meet you too, Zabby," he said in a nervous voice.

"Hey, pal, we're gonna sing some Christmas tunes...how 'bout you join us?!" Jagger asked as he put his arm around Walter, and led him toward the others.

Walter was too shy to sing along, but said he would like to listen to the other monsters sing. They gathered around, and sang as loudly as they could.

Walter watched and listened as the monsters happily sang their Christmas songs. "This must be what Christmas is all about," he thought to himself.

After the singing was over, Clem grabbed one of the gifts that was waiting near the tree. "Time for preseeents!" he yelled.

TO: LARRY
FROM: CLEM

"This is my favorite part!" Jagger exclaimed. All of the monsters stood in a circle, and exchanged gifts to each other.

They eagerly ripped off the bows and wrapping paper to discover what was inside. As gifts were opened, they thanked each other for such wonderful surprises.

Walter was getting a little confused. He thought to himself, "I guess Christmas is all about cocoa, songs, decorations, and presents."

Larry looked around the room with joy in his heart. He was so happy to see his friends having a good time. But he also noticed that Walter had not joined in any of the fun. He decided to go talk to him.

"This definitely is my favorite time of the year," said Larry. Walter replied, "This is really nice, Larry. Thanks again for inviting me here."

"I guess Christmas is about decorations, presents, and cocoa," Walter said. "I can see why everyone is so happy."

"Well, all of those things are nice," said Larry. "That's true. And those things help us share our joy and our spirit with others. But the most important thing about Christmas is celebrating time and love with our family and friends. Giving is so important. No decoration or gift can ever replace that. Today you gave us all the best gift anyone could ever give...the gift of your friendship."

Larry then gave Walter something he had never received before—a gift. " This is my way of sharing our friendship, Walter," Larry said. *"Merry Christmas!"*

Walter didn't know what to say. "Why is this monster being so nice to me? What have I done to deserve this kindness?" he thought to himself.

Walter held the present in his hands. He felt a warmth grow inside of him. It was something special, something he had never felt before.

Walter looked up and saw all of the monsters—Jagger, Zabby, Sanford, Clem, Xola, and Xue—standing in front of him. Each had a gift to give.

Walter couldn't believe how nice these strangers were. His eyes teared up with joy.

Surrounded by presents, and his new friends, Walter cried some happy tears.

He looked up at the beautiful Christmas tree in front of him. The joy of Christmas filled his heart, and he finally knew what Christmas was really all about.

Walter gave Larry a big, warm hug and thanked him for such a wonderful day. For the first time in his life, he did not feel alone.

Jagger was also filled with the Christmas spirit and grabbed up Larry and Walter. "A new friend for Christmas," he roared, "Can't get any better than that!"

Surrounded by his new friends, Walter's heart was warm and his spirit was renewed. And he finally understood. Being with friends and family...*that's* what Christmas is really all about.